The Perfect Pal

by Jack Gantos and Nicole Rubel

Houghton Mifflin Company   Boston   1979

To my grandmother

J.G.

To my brother, David

N.R.

Library of Congress Cataloging in Publication Data

Gantos, Jack.
    The perfect pal.

    SUMMARY: Wendell, the pet store salesman, helps
Vanessa to find just the right pal for her.
    [1. Animals – Fiction. 2. Pets – Fiction]
I. Rubel, Nicole. II. Title.
PZ7.G15334Pe   [E]   79-12310

ISBN 0-395-28380-9

One morning Vanessa didn't have a smile
on her face.
"What I need is a pal to cheer me up," she
said to herself.
She knew just where to find one.

She went straight to the pet shop.

"May I help you?" asked Wendell, the sales assistant.

"I'm looking for a cheerful pet that will make a good pal," said Vanessa.

"Fish are very nice," Wendell suggested.

"I'm looking for something I could have milk and cookies with," explained Vanessa.

"A pig would be ideal for milk and cookies," said Wendell.

"I'll take it," decided Vanessa.

"You just make yourself comfortable," Vanessa said
to the pig when she arrived home. "I'm going to fix us a
nice snack."

But when the milk and cookies were served the pig
became very excited. It jumped on the table and
ate everything right up.

"Mind your manners!" ordered Vanessa.

"Oink!" burped the pig. Then it wiped its mouth
on the tablecloth.

Vanessa put the pig in her bathroom and returned

to the pet shop. "That pig won't make a good pal," she

said to Wendell. "Its table manners are horrid."

"A good pal must have good manners," agreed Wendell.

Just then the alarm rang to wake the sloth.

"Now there is a calm, well-behaved animal," remarked

Vanessa.

"Perhaps a little too calm and well-behaved,"

added Wendell.

"It seems just fine for me," replied Vanessa.

Wendell placed the sloth in her arms. Already it

had fallen back to sleep.

That afternoon Vanessa wanted to go dancing.

"I'll take my new pal and we'll have a grand time,"
she thought.

She dressed the sloth in a little coat and placed a
bow tie around its neck. It looked quite handsome.

But the sloth was a terrible bore. It slept through
every dance.

"This snoring sloth is no fun," Vanessa said.

Then she carried it home and tucked it into bed.

Wendell was cleaning the parrot cage when Vanessa entered the shop.

"Hello again," she said.

"Howdy," replied Wendell. "What's the problem?"

"That sloth was just too sleepy for me," she explained. "I took it to a dance, and all it did was snore."

"Perhaps a talking parrot might be more lively," he suggested.

"I like snappy conversation," said Vanessa.

"So do I," replied Wendell. Then he placed the parrot on her shoulder.

But at the soda shop Vanessa and the parrot
didn't have a nice conversation.

"Hello dummy!" it said to the waiter.

Then it flew across the room and landed on a
woman's hat.

"This is the ugliest hat I've ever sat on!" it
squawked.

Vanessa was horrified. She quickly grabbed the
parrot and ran out of the soda shop.

Vanessa put the parrot in a cage. Then she returned to the pet shop.

"That parrot is too unkind to be my pal," she explained.

"There is no excuse for insulting behavior," said Wendell.

"What I want is a friendly pet that would be good company," said Vanessa.

"That's the best kind," agreed Wendell. "How about a sheep dog?"

"What a fine choice," said Vanessa. She took the dog right away.

But when Vanessa took the friendly sheep dog for a

rowboat ride she found out that it wasn't a good choice.

It couldn't sit still for a minute.

It kept scratching its fleas and hopping up and

down. It rocked the boat back and forth and almost

tipped it over.

"This flea-bitten sheep dog can't relax," cried

Vanessa. Then as fast as she could she took it home and

put it in her backyard.

"I'm sorry for bothering you again," said Vanessa when she returned to the pet shop, "but I've decided I'd rather have a more relaxed pet for a pal."

"How about a snake?" suggested Wendell, who tried his best to be helpful.

"No, thank you," replied Vanessa. Then she saw the hermit crab. It had such a beautiful shell. "That's just what I'm looking for," said Vanessa. "A quiet, beautiful pet to keep me company."

"Be careful," said Wendell. "It's not as nice as it looks."

"Nonsense," replied Vanessa. Then she left the shop.

When Vanessa arrived home she was very tired.

"Looking for a good pal is exhausting." She yawned.

"I must take a nap."

But when she lay down the hermit crab crept up

and pinched her on the toe.

"Ouch!" yelled Vanessa. "What a sneaky pet."

She jumped up and put the hermit crab in a bucket.

"I could never get any rest with a pal like this

around the house."

Once more she returned to the pet shop.

"You were right," Vanessa said to Wendell. "That hermit crab wasn't as nice as it looked."

"A little time will always tell a good pal from a bad one," said Wendell.

"Perhaps a monkey would be perfect," said Vanessa, noticing it for the first time.

"They are almost human," explained Wendell.

"In that case I'll take it," Vanessa decided.

But the monkey ignored Vanessa and played with all
the other animals.
Vanessa felt less cheerful than when she didn't
have any pals at all.

"I've had enough of these imperfect pals!"

shouted Vanessa.

"An unmannered pig that's too messy!

"A sloth that's a sleepyhead!

"A parrot that's insulting!

"A flea-bitten sheep dog that can't relax!

"A pinching crab that's not as nice as it looks!

"And a monkey that plays with everyone but me!"

There was only one thing left to do.

Wendell was just closing the shop when Vanessa returned with all her pets.

"Greetings," said Wendell.

"After trying all these pets," said Vanessa, "I've decided I can't find a pal."

"But there is still one you haven't tried," said Wendell.

"What's that?" asked Vanessa.

"Me!" said Wendell. "I'm your perfect pal!"

"Why didn't I think of you sooner?" said Vanessa.

"You're well mannered, wide awake, polite,

relaxed, attentive, and you don't pretend

to be something you are not."

"And I think you are perfect, too," said Wendell.